.357 SUNSET

THE REACHER EXPERIMENT BOOK 5

Jude Hardin

January 2018

1

What kind of idiot tries to steal a piano?

A baby grand.

Wide as a car.

Rock Wahlman stood there in the ankle-deep water, trying to wrap his head around the absurdity of such a thing. He'd been walking along the alley that ran parallel to Sunset Road, minding his own business, heading two blocks west toward the main thoroughfare, taking a shortcut to a place he'd been told was a good place to get something to eat, when he'd heard a trickling sound and had turned his head enough to notice that a set of French doors on the back of one of the houses was standing wide open.

When he'd walked up to the doors and peeked in, it was immediately obvious that water was leaking into the house from somewhere, and when he'd stepped inside and started looking around, it was immediately obvious that a wall had been partially demolished with a sledgehammer, and that a copper pipe had been severely damaged in the process.

No furniture in the house, other than the piano. The

thief—or team of thieves, probably, the more Wahlman thought about it—had been trying to push the bulky instrument from one room to another, moving it closer to the French doors, closer to the alley, where a truck was probably waiting. They'd busted the wall apart in an attempt to widen the interior doorway.

Not a bad plan, Wahlman supposed, as far as dumbass plans devised by dumbass people went, but apparently the dumbass people had given up when the water had started gushing out of the broken pipe.

"Hands on your head," a male voice from behind Wahlman shouted. "Turn around and face me. Slowly."

"I was just trying to—"

"Hands on your head, asshole. Now!"

Wahlman didn't like being told what to do, and he didn't like being called an asshole. But the man had him at a disadvantage. From the sound of the man's voice, Wahlman figured he was standing approximately ten feet away from where Wahlman was standing. Wahlman was a very large man, and he had a very long reach. But not that long. The man standing behind him spoke authoritatively. Unwaveringly. Probably a cop, Wahlman thought. Probably aiming his service weapon in the general direction of Wahlman's heart.

Wahlman laced his fingers together behind his head, turned around slowly and faced the man, who was indeed a cop, and who was indeed standing approximately ten feet from where Wahlman was standing, and who was indeed aiming the fat barrel of a semi-automatic pistol in the general direction of Wahlman's heart.

The man wore a dark blue uniform. There was a silver badge pinned over his left breast pocket, and a black microphone attached to his right epaulet. Black patent leather holster. Wahlman figured he had matching shoes, but it was impossible to tell for sure at the moment, because they were covered with four or five inches of smelly gray water.

The engraved banner at the top of the officer's badge said RPD. Reality Police Department. The plastic nameplate above the banner said Hurt.

"I can explain," Wahlman said.

"Shut up," Officer Hurt said.

He keyed his mic, identified himself to the dispatcher, and requested backup. Breaking and entering, he said. Three fifty-seven Sunset Road. One suspect, currently being detained at gunpoint.

A few minutes later, three more officers showed up.

A few minutes after that, Wahlman was sitting in the back of Officer Hurt's police car with his hands cuffed behind his back. The door Wahlman had been forced into, the door on the rear passenger side, had been left open, and the four officers were standing a few feet away, talking about something in hushed tones.

Wahlman had spent twenty years as a Master-At-Arms in the United States Navy. So he had a pretty good idea of what Hurt and the other guys were talking about. They were probably discussing whether or not they had enough evidence against Wahlman to actually arrest him. If they thought they did, Officer Hurt, who had been first on the scene, would probably read Wahlman his rights and then drive him to the station for processing. If they thought they didn't, Officer Hurt would probably remove the handcuffs and send Wahlman on his merry way.

Officer Hurt turned and stepped closer to the car.

"What were you doing inside the house?" he said.

"I was trying to find the main water valve," Wahlman said. "I was going to shut it off."

"Why?"

"Seemed like the neighborly thing to do."

"You live around here? Is that what you're saying?"

"I'm saying it seemed like the neighborly thing to do. You can do something neighborly without actually being a neighbor."

"Why don't you have any identification with you?" Hurt said.

"I already answered that question. Right after your friend over there patted me down."

"Answer it again."

"I left my wallet in my car," Wahlman said.

Which was a lie. Wahlman had actually left the wallet in his hotel room, but he didn't want the police to know that he had such easy access to it. Once your phony driver's license got scanned and put into the system, you pretty much had to get a new one right away. And the good ones were expensive.

"Where's your car?" Officer Hurt said.

"Reality Auto Repair. Sunset and Fifth. They were closing up just as I left. I took one of their business cards from a stack on the counter. It was in my front pocket. Your friend over there took it. I need it back."

Wahlman had been traveling west on the interstate when his SUV broke down. He'd been planning on making it through Missouri and into Kansas before dark, but the engine had started making a strange rattling sound, and then it had quit running altogether. Back in the day when most people still used cell phones on a regular basis, most people would have stayed with the vehicle and called for a tow truck. But those days were long gone. Cell phones were still around. Some people still carried them. Most didn't. Wary of the growing number of hackers out to steal their lives, most people had reverted to landlines in their homes, and most people had started using payphones if they needed to make calls while they were out. Wahlman hadn't owned a cell phone in a long time, and he certainly wouldn't have been carrying one now that he was on the run. Too easy to hack, too easy to track, as the old saying went. So when his car had broken down, Wahlman had pulled to the shoulder and had climbed out of the vehicle and had walked to the nearest exit.

There had been a sign at the bottom of the ramp, with two arrows painted on it. One of the arrows pointed east, and the other pointed west.

The arrow that pointed east said *FANTASY 1.4 MILES.*

The one that pointed west said *REALITY 1.3 MILES.*

Wahlman had chosen Reality. It was a tenth of a mile closer, for one thing, and it was west of where he'd broken down, which would put him that much closer to Kansas once his SUV was towed in and repaired.

The people over at Reality Auto Repair had seemed very nice, and the people at the hotel across the street had seemed very nice, but now Wahlman was starting to wish that he'd walked in the opposite direction.

Reality was getting a little hard to deal with at the moment.

"What's wrong with your car?" Officer Hurt said.

"I don't know," Wahlman said. "I'm not a mechanic."

"What are you?"

"Just a guy."

"What's that supposed to mean?"

"It's not supposed to mean anything."

"What's your name?"

"I already answered that question too."

"Answer it again."

Wahlman gave Officer Hurt the same fake name he'd given the officer who'd searched him earlier. The officer who'd searched him earlier was named Tingly. Short and round and balding. Sergeant's stripes. Thick brown mustache, littered with some powdery remnants of the doughnut he'd been eating when he'd gotten the call to come for backup.

Tingly was still standing a few feet away from Officer Hurt's cruiser, standing there with the other two guys, the three of them laughing about something now.

Wahlman didn't know the names of the other two guys. He'd never gotten close enough to them to read their nameplates.

"Must be a slow crime day in Reality," Wahlman said, nodding toward the jolly trio.

"Where do you live?" Hurt said.

"The Reality Hotel. Sunset and Fifth. Right across the street from—"

"I know where it is," Hurt said. "I need a home address."

"I'm currently between residences," Wahlman said.

"You mean you're moving somewhere?"

"You could say that."

"Where?"

"I was on my way to Kansas when I broke down."

"Why were you walking down this particular alley, at this particular time of the evening?"

"Because this is the United States of America, and I'm allowed to do that."

Officer Hurt nodded. He turned and stepped over to where the other three officers were standing. Tingly and the other two guys. A couple of minutes later, Officer Hurt walked back over to the cruiser and helped Wahlman out and removed the cuffs.

"We're going to let you off with a warning this time," he said, handing over the folded wad of cash that Tingly had taken from Wahlman's front pocket, along with the business card from Reality Auto Repair.

"What are you warning me not to do?" Wahlman said.

"I'm warning you not to be a smartass, for one thing. And I'm warning you not to walk into houses that aren't yours."

"What if I'm invited into a house that isn't mine?"

"What did I just say about not being a smartass?"

Wahlman shrugged. He massaged some circulation back into his wrists, and then he proceeded toward the place he'd been told was a good place to get something to eat.

2

Wahlman sat at the counter. Not on the stool closest to the door, but the one next to that. He didn't like being on the very end. There never seemed to be enough elbow room. A waitress gave him a menu and a glass of ice water and she walked away and came back a couple of minutes later and he ordered a double bacon cheeseburger. Well-done, fully dressed, mayonnaise on the side. He ordered the platter, which came with fries and coleslaw and a drink.

Any drink you wanted, any size.

Wahlman wanted coffee.

"What size?" the waitress said.

She was holding a ballpoint pen and a pad of guest checks. Old school. Like something you might see in a classic film.

"This is not a to-go order," Wahlman said. "I'm going to eat here."

He looked to see if the waitress was wearing a nametag. She wasn't. She was young. Twenty-one, maybe twenty-two. She had blue eyes and light brown hair and perfect teeth. She was working the counter by herself. It was dinnertime, and the place was busy, but everyone except Wahlman was sitting at a table or a booth. Which meant that he pretty much had her to himself for the moment. A nice relaxed situation, ordinarily. But it didn't seem that way. There was a tenseness about the waitress. A sense of urgency. As if there were ten customers sitting at the counter instead of just one.

"I still need to know what size coffee you want," she said, thumbing the clicker on her ballpoint pen.

Nervously.

Repeatedly.

Annoyingly.

"I want a ceramic mug," Wahlman said. "Whatever size that is. And I want you to come and fill it for me every time it gets close to being empty."

"That's not how it works here," the waitress said.

"How does it work here?"

"We have paper cups. You can get any size you want with the platter you ordered, but if you want more after that, it costs extra."

Wahlman thought about that. He figured The Reality Diner served hundreds of drinks every day. Which meant that hundreds of paper cups were being tossed into the trashcan every day. It seemed very wasteful. Not to mention that a number of the cups probably ended up on the side of the highway.

"This is the first diner I've ever been to that doesn't serve coffee in real cups," Wahlman said.

"They're real cups," the waitress said. "They're just made out of paper."

"Is there another restaurant around here?"

"You want to cancel your order?"

"No. Just wondering."

"There's a place over in Fantasy."

"Do they serve coffee in paper cups?"

"I don't know. I've never been there."

"I guess I'll take a large," Wahlman said. "What's your name?"

"We're not allowed to tell customers our names," the waitress said. "Sorry. You want cream and sugar with that?"

"No thanks. Is there a payphone here somewhere?"

"Outside. By the newspaper machines."

Wahlman got up and walked outside. He pulled the business card out of his pocket, slid some coins into the phone, and punched in the number. A man picked up after four rings.

"Reality Auto," the man said.

"I was calling to check on my car," Wahlman said.

"Which one is yours?"

"The white SUV."

"You need a fuel pump."

"Okay. What time do you think you'll have it done?"

The man laughed. "We closed an hour ago," he said. "Technically, I'm not even supposed to be answering the phone this late."

"Are you the guy I talked to a while ago?"

"That's me."

"So what happened?"

Earlier, Wahlman had offered to pay the man extra money to perform the repair right away. A hundred dollars. Sort of a bonus. Straight from Wahlman's pocket to the man's pocket. The man had agreed to those terms. He'd wanted the money up front, and Wahlman had given it to him. The man had promised to get the job done, even if it took until midnight.

"Couldn't get the part," the man said. "I put in a special order. Should be here sometime in the morning. At least by lunchtime. But we're kind of backed up right now, so—"

"I need to be in Junction City by two o'clock tomorrow afternoon," Wahlman said.

"Don't know what to tell you," the man said.

Wahlman had been searching for information pertaining to an army colonel who went by the name of Dorland. It was a codename. Wahlman knew that much. It had to be, because Wahlman had searched every military database available to the public, and there weren't any officers currently on active duty with that last name.

Which meant that Wahlman needed to gain access to the army's restricted databases.

Which meant that he needed passwords.

He'd set up a meeting with a professional hacker, a civilian who worked part time in one of the offices at Fort Riley. The guy hadn't made any promises, and he hadn't given Wahlman any details about how the exchange of information was going to work. That was what the meeting was supposed to be about. The guy refused to discuss the matter over the phone or online.

Which was understandable.

The guy would be taking a huge risk if he ended up actually doing what Wahlman wanted him to do.

Now it was starting to look like the meeting wasn't even going to happen, because it was starting to look like a fuel pump wasn't going to happen. Not tonight, anyway. Special order, the man had said.

"What about my hundred dollars?" Wahlman said.

"What hundred dollars?" the man said.

Wahlman thought about ripping the receiver away from the steel-coated cable it was attached to and carrying it over to Reality Auto Repair and shoving it up the man's ass. But he didn't. He calmly told the man that he would stop by in the morning to discuss the matter further, and then he hung up the phone.

Now the man would have all night to think about it. Maybe he would decide to give Wahlman the money back on his own. Or maybe he would need a certain amount of persuasion. Either way, Wahlman wasn't leaving Reality until the cash he'd given the man was back in his pocket.

He walked back into the diner and sat on the same stool he'd been sitting on earlier. He'd been hoping that the food he'd ordered would be waiting for him, but it wasn't. The Waitress With No Name hadn't even poured him any coffee yet. She was talking to a pair of guys at the other end of the counter. Both of the guys were wearing jeans and flannel shirts and ball caps, and neither of them had shaved in a while. They were older than the waitress, but younger than Wahlman. Late twenties, early thirties. Wahlman figured they'd walked in while he was on the phone.

The waitress glanced over at Wahlman, and then she turned back around and held up an index finger to let the guys she'd been talking to know that she would be right back. She walked to Wahlman's end of the counter and asked him if he still wanted coffee.

"Why wouldn't I?" Wahlman said.

"Just checking," the waitress said. "I didn't know if you were coming back or not."

She rattled off another staccato series of clicks with the ballpoint pen. Wahlman tried not to look as aggravated as he felt. The waitress poured some coffee into a gigantic insulated paper cup and set it on the counter in front of him.

"I still want the double cheeseburger platter too," he said.

The waitress nodded. She jotted the order down on her pad, and then she turned around and tapped her finger on a computer screen a few times. Relaying the order to a monitor screen back in the kitchen, Wahlman supposed. Or a printer. Or whatever. When she finished tapping on the screen, she walked back over to where the flannel shirt guys were sitting. The guys had paper cups in front of them, identical to Wahlman's, except theirs had lids. The waitress leaned over the counter toward the guy on the left, and he leaned over the counter toward her, and they kissed on the lips. Then both of the guys got up and headed toward the door.

Wahlman watched them as they exited the restaurant.

The man who hadn't kissed the waitress was wearing black leather work boots. Well worn, but not worn out.

The man who had kissed the waitress was wearing work boots too. But his weren't black. They were tan. Khaki. The shade of sand in the desert.

Similar to the ones Wahlman was wearing.

And, similar to the ones Wahlman was wearing, they were wet up to the ankles.

3

It was the kind of place people sometimes referred to as a hole in the wall. Depending on the time of day you pushed your way through the heavily-tinted steel and glass door, you might see a wrinkled old drunk slumping over a shot glass or a middle-aged couple meeting for an extramarital highball or a cluster of restaurant workers drinking beer and complaining about how busy or how slow their shifts had been.

Jackson P. Feldman didn't see any of that. He was the only customer at the moment. He limped up to the bar, his left knee still bothering him from an injury he'd sustained in Bakersfield, California. He usually told people that he'd been playing tennis out there in the desert, trying to get back in shape, but that wasn't the truth. Jackson P. Feldman hadn't played tennis in years, and getting back in shape was the furthest thing from his mind these days. The truth was, he'd gotten his ass kicked by a man named Rock Wahlman, a fugitive from justice he'd been hired to locate.

"What can I get for you?" the bartender said.

"Bourbon on the rocks," Feldman said. "Make it a double."

Feldman figured the bartender was probably in his early twenties. He wore black pants and a black polo shirt and a tooled leather belt with a fancy silver buckle on it. Light brown hair, buzzed short on the back and sides. Like a military cut. You could tell he spent some time at the gym. Not too much, just enough. He was toned, but not musclebound. Clean. Quick. Balanced. He grabbed a short heavy glass from a shelf behind the bar, dropped a couple of ice cubes in it with a pair of tongs, picked up a bottle of inexpensive but fairly respectable Kentucky bourbon whiskey from the stainless steel well rack at his knees, poured a generous amount of the amber liquid into the glass. Counting off the seconds in his head with the red plastic speed pourer attached to the neck of the bottle, Feldman supposed, rather than using any sort of precise measuring device. Bar owners weren't especially fond of that sort of technique, but customers were, because they tended to get a little more liquor than they were paying for. Which frequently resulted in a bigger tip for the man or woman doing the pouring.

The man doing the pouring at this particular establishment slapped a cocktail napkin on the bar in front of Feldman, and then he gently set the drink on the napkin.

"You want to start a tab?" he said.

"Sure," Feldman said, handing the young man his credit card.

Feldman had been wearing a brace on the knee, but it

still hurt. Really bad sometimes. Alcohol was the only thing that seemed to keep the pain at bay. Feldman knew that he should have seen a doctor the day he'd sustained the injury, knew that he should have gone to the emergency room and had x-rays and all that, but he hadn't wanted to take the time. And he didn't like doctors. The ER physician probably would have referred him to a surgeon, and the surgeon probably would have wanted to operate. And that just wasn't going to happen. Feldman didn't have the time, and he didn't have the money. He figured the joint would eventually heal on its own. In the meantime, there was whiskey.

He took a long pull from the glass in front of him.

There was a television mounted on the wall behind the bar. The bartender picked up a remote control and started clicking through channels.

"Let me know if you see anything you want to watch," he said.

Feldman rarely watched television, because there was rarely anything on it that he wanted to see. It was a waste of time, as far as he was concerned. But he didn't tell the bartender that.

"Someone's supposed to meet me here at six," he said. "We'll probably move to a booth. So watch whatever you want."

The bartender shrugged, set the remote back beside the plastic napkin caddy at the edge of the bar, where it had been before he picked it up. He'd stopped on an old situation comedy from the middle of the twentieth century. Which, in Feldman's opinion, was the only time in history that television had been very entertaining. He glanced up at the screen for a few seconds, but the volume was too low for him to hear any of the dialogue.

"You a cop?" the bartender said.

"What makes you think that?" Feldman said, caught off guard by the question.

"I don't know. You just have the look. Not that I have anything against cops. They come in here all the time."

"I'm not a cop," Feldman said. "But I used to be one."

"Retired?"

"Yeah."

Feldman didn't see any point in telling the bartender any more than that. The fact that he was one of the most respected private investigators in the country was none of the bartender's business.

Feldman drained the last of the bourbon from his glass, nodded for the bartender to give him a refill.

"You want some pretzels or anything?" the bartender said, pouring another double over the same ice cubes.

"No thanks," Feldman said.

A sudden wedge of temporary brightness flooded the room as a tall and thin man entered and made his way over to where Feldman was sitting. The tall and thin man was wearing jeans and a western-style shirt and cowboy boots. He looked like he was going to a rodeo. All he needed was a hat. He had a fresh haircut and a clean shave and he smelled like some kind of cologne you might pick up at a grocery store.

"You Feldman?" he said.

"Yes," Feldman said.

"I'm Decker. Let's talk over here."

Feldman picked up his drink and climbed off of the stool he'd been sitting on and followed Decker to the far right corner of the room, to the booth furthest from the bar. Decker sat with his back to the wall, facing the door. Feldman slid into the seat across from him, trying not to grimace as an electric spear of agony traveled from his knee to the top of his scalp.

"You don't want anything to drink?" Feldman said.

"I don't drink," Decker said, unsnapping one of his shirt pockets and pulling out a pen and a notepad. "What did you want to talk to me about?"

"I wanted to talk to you about tracking a guy."

"I figured that. It's what I do. Tell me the particulars, and I'll let you know if I might be able to help you."

"The guy I'm looking for is a suspect in a murder case," Feldman said. "His name is Rock Wahlman. He's six feet four inches tall, and he weighs—"

"Who hired you to find him?"

"A detective named Collins. Down in New Orleans."

"So you're being paid by the NOPD?"

"Correct."

"And who's going to be paying me?"

"I am," Feldman said. "Out of my own pocket."

"I told you my rate over the phone. You're good with that?"

"I'm good with it."

"Why don't you just find this Wahlman guy yourself?" Decker said.

"I was a police officer for twenty years," Feldman said. "I've been a private investigator for a little over seven. If there's one thing I've learned, it's that there's no shame in asking for help when you need it. Wahlman's smart, and he's deadly, and he doesn't want to be caught. He's getting money from somewhere, substantial amounts of cash for travel expenses and fake driver's licenses and whatnot. No paper trail. At least I haven't been able to find one."

"Any idea where he's getting the money?"

"He was traveling with a woman named Kasey Stielson. Her family's pretty well-off. I think they might be funding his current lifestyle."

Decker wrote something on the notepad. Feldman took a swallow of whiskey.

"When you say family, you mean her parents?" Decker said.

"Yes," Feldman said. "Her parents."

"Got an address for them?"

"I do. I have their home address, but they're not living there right now. It's like they abandoned the place. That's one of the problems. I have no idea where they went."

"Tell me the address," Decker said.

Feldman told him the street number and zip code. Decker wrote it all down.

"The house is only a few miles from here," Feldman said. "But they might have left the country for all I know."

"I doubt it. You said they're rich. They probably have

another house somewhere. I'm assuming you checked the county real estate records for a second address."

"I did," Feldman said. "If they have another house, it's not in Davidson County. I ran a national search on one of the databases I subscribe to, came up with nothing."

"How current is the database?"

"They update it twice a year. I guess it's possible that—"

"Right. I have access to a national real estate site that gets updated weekly. It's expensive, but it's worth it. Especially for someone in my line of work. I use it all the time."

Feldman knew about the database Decker was referring to. He'd tried it for a while, found it to be unreliable about half the time. But maybe it had gotten better. He decided not to say anything negative about it for the moment.

"If you can find Kasey's parents, that would be a good start," he said.

"I'll find them," Decker said. "Their name's Stielson?"

"No. Kasey was married to a guy named Stielson. He was shot in his car out in the Mojave Desert, but we don't think—"

"What's the name of the people I'm looking for?" Decker said.

"Lennik," Feldman said. "Dean and Betsy."

"Dean and Betsy Lennik. Got it. Does Kasey have any other relatives I should know about?"

"She has a daughter."

"Name?"

"Natalie. She's a minor. Fourteen. Same last name as her mom. Stielson."

"Great. Now tell me all about the murder suspect you're trying to track down."

Feldman took another drink of whiskey, and then he told Decker everything he knew about Rock Wahlman.

4

There were a million different ways the man who'd kissed the waitress could have gotten his boots wet. Perhaps he'd stepped in a puddle of rainwater. Or maybe he'd been fishing from a leaky boat. Maybe he installed sprinkler systems for a living.

There were a million different ways.

It seemed highly unlikely that he'd been involved in the situation over at 357 Sunset.

Highly unlikely, but possible.

Wahlman tried to shrug it off. It was none of his business. He had things to do. Pressing matters to take care of.

The Waitress With No Name brought the double bacon cheeseburger and the fries and the coleslaw.

"Is there a bus station around here anywhere?" Wahlman said.

"I don't know if you'd really call it a station, but there's a little shack where a guy sells tickets. Two blocks west, right on the corner."

"Okay. Thanks."

"Where you heading?"

"Junction City. I have an appointment tomorrow afternoon. My car's in the shop, and it doesn't look like it's going to be finished in time."

"So you're going to Junction City, and then you're coming back here?"

"Looks that way."

The Waitress with No Name nodded.

"Junction City isn't that far," she said. "My boyfriend could probably give you a ride in his truck. It wouldn't be free, but it would be cheaper than taking a bus."

"What makes you think your boyfriend would want to do that?" Wahlman said.

"He's out of work right now. He could use the money."

Wahlman thought about it. A ride in a personal vehicle would be more convenient than a ride on a bus. And more comfortable. And less expensive. But Wahlman didn't want to get involved with any of the locals in Reality, Missouri. He didn't want to get involved with any of the locals anywhere. He needed to be as anonymous as possible, talk to as few people as possible.

"Thanks anyway, but I think I'll take the bus," he said.

"Okay. Suit yourself."

The Waitress With No Name turned and walked away. There was a phone on the wall, a couple of feet to the right of the coffeemakers. She picked up the receiver and punched in a number and started talking to someone.

Whispering.

Wahlman couldn't hear what she was saying, and he didn't care what she was saying. He squirted some ketchup on his plate, dragged a French fry through it, and took a bite.

5

The bus station was exactly as The Waitress With No Name had described it. A shack on the corner. More like a miniature hut. There wasn't enough room for two regular-sized people to fit in there, and there wasn't enough room for one Wahlman-sized person to fit in there. It reminded Wahlman of a structure he'd seen in a history book one time, where people dropped photographic film off to be processed. You put your name and address on an envelope and sealed your roll of film in there and the attendant told you how many days it would be until your pictures were ready. Hard to imagine. Like traveling across the country in a covered wagon or something. Just unfathomably slow.

A woman with long blonde hair and a nice smile slid the window open when she saw Wahlman approaching.

"Can I help you?" she said.

"I need to get to Junction City, Kansas," Wahlman said. "Tonight, if possible."

The woman tapped the monitor screen in front of her with a nicely manicured fingernail a few times, and then she consulted a three-ring binder that was bulging with printouts.

"There's a coach coming in from New York City, headed toward Topeka. It'll be here tomorrow afternoon, a little after one if it's running on time. From Topeka you can connect to—"

"That's too late," Wahlman said. "I need to be in Junction City by one or one-thirty. Two at the latest."

"Oh. Then I don't know what to tell you."

"Where's the nearest airport?"

"There's an airstrip over in Fantasy. But they don't land any passenger planes over there or anything. Just those little ones people buzz around in for fun."

"Where's the nearest real airport?" Wahlman said.

"Jefferson City."

"How soon can a bus get me there?"

The woman tapped the screen some more and paged through the binder some more.

"That coach should be coming through here around noon tomorrow," she said. "But even if you were able to get a flight out of Jefferson City right away—"

"So you're telling me that there's no way you can get me to Junction City by two o'clock tomorrow afternoon?"

"Sorry. A bus left here for Topeka about fifteen minutes ago. Too bad you didn't stop by a little sooner."

"Yeah," Wahlman said. "Too bad."

He walked back down to the diner, sat on the same stool. The Waitress With No Name was standing over by the coffee machine, sorting silverware and rolling it into paper napkins. When she turned to carry a handful of the wrapped utensils over to the bin where they were being stored, she saw Wahlman sitting there.

"You're back," she said.

"Could I get another large coffee, please?"

"Sure."

The waitress lowered the silverware into the bin, walked back over to the coffee setup and filled one of the gigantic paper cups. She set it on the counter in front of Wahlman. It was hot and it smelled fresh.

"Thanks," Wahlman said.

"How did it go at the bus station?"

"Not so good."

"Sorry to hear that."

"I was wondering if your boyfriend might still be interested in giving me a ride," Wahlman said.

"I can give him a call and ask, if you want me to."

"Yes. I would appreciate that."

The Waitress With No Name stepped over to the telephone and punched in a number. Started whispering again. A few seconds later, she hung up and walked back over to where Wahlman was sitting.

"He's on his way over here," she said.

"Great," Wahlman said.

He sipped his coffee and waited. The coffee was fresh, but it had a faint aftertaste he hadn't noticed earlier. Like the glue on the flap of an envelope when you lick it.

Wahlman had thought about walking up to the highway and hitchhiking, but that was always hit or miss. Especially with a man Wahlman's size. He was six feet four inches tall, and he weighed two hundred and thirty pounds. Chest muscles as big as frying pans, abs like a six-pack of sledgehammer heads. He looked like the kind of guy who could break you in half if he wanted to. And he was that kind of guy. Not that he ever went looking for trouble. He didn't. But motorists tended to shy away when he walked along the shoulder with his thumb out, sometimes to the point of changing lanes to maximize the distance, as if he might reach out and yank them from their seats as they whizzed by at eighty miles an hour.

Hitchhiking was always an option, but it was one that Wahlman avoided for the most part. The meeting with the hacker in Junction City tomorrow was too important to risk missing. It was probably Wahlman's best chance at identifying and locating the army colonel who'd been trying to kill him, at getting to the bottom of why all this was happening. Wahlman needed to be there on time, and he needed a mode of transportation that would be more dependable than hitchhiking.

The Boyfriend of The Waitress With No Name walked into the restaurant. He'd changed clothes. He wasn't wearing the tan boots anymore. Different shirt, different jeans. He walked up to the counter and sat down, leaving one stool between him and Wahlman.

"You the guy who needs a ride?" he said.

"Yes," Wahlman said.

"What's your name?"

"Is it important?"

"I guess not. We can just remain anonymous as far as I'm concerned. You ready to go now?"

"My meeting's at two o'clock tomorrow afternoon," Wahlman said. "After the meeting, I'm going to need a ride back to Reality."

"We can leave at ten tomorrow morning if you want to," The Boyfriend Of The Waitress With No Name said. "That should give you plenty of time."

"And you'll wait around for me, and then bring me back?"

"Sure."

"How much?"

Boyfriend gave Wahlman a price. It was a little steep, but Wahlman wasn't in a position to haggle.

"I'll meet you here at the diner at ten in the morning," Boyfriend said.

"Okay," Wahlman said. "Is there a place around here where I can buy a phone?"

"Yeah. About a mile from here. It's on my way home. I can drop you off if you want me to."

"I would appreciate that."

Wahlman requested a lid for his cup, and then he followed Boyfriend out to the parking lot.

6

Wahlman bought a cheap little disposable flip-top cell phone—the kind you use for a few days and then crush with the heel of your boot. He activated the device, and then he walked to the hotel and called Kasey from his room. She was still staying at her parents' lake house in Tennessee. It had been a couple of days since Wahlman had talked to her.

"Where are you?" she said.

"Missouri," Wahlman said, always careful not to be very specific about his location, in case someone was listening in. Unlikely, but there was no point in taking any chances.

Kasey knew the drill.

"I thought you would be further west by now," she said.

"The SUV broke down. I had to have it towed."

"You need money?"

"No. I have enough for now."

"Are you sure?"

"I'm sure."

"Are you still planning to meet with that guy tomorrow afternoon?"

"My car's not going to be ready in time. I'm paying someone to drive me."

"You think you're going to be able to get the information you need?" Kasey said.

"I hope so."

"I hope so too. I'm not sure how much more of this I can take."

Kasey's tone had changed abruptly. She sounded anxious. Distraught.

"How much more of what?" Wahlman said.

"Being separated like this. I don't know. Just the uncertainty of it all."

Wahlman had left his home in Florida and had been out on the road for months. Literally running for his life. He loved Kasey, and he wanted to be with her, but he couldn't just hide out there at her parents' lake house forever, as she had previously suggested. He was afraid that his troubles might follow him there, for one thing, putting Kasey and her family in great danger. He needed to find out why he had been targeted, and he needed to figure out a way to put a stop to it.

And he needed to do it alone.

Then he could deal with the charges that had been brought against him in New Orleans. Then maybe he and Kasey could have a chance at some kind of life together.

"I'm doing the best I can," he said.

"I know you are. It's just that—"

"Everything's going to work out. I just need a little more time."

There was a long pause.

"There's someone at the door," Kasey said. "Call me tomorrow and let me know how it goes, okay?"

"Okay," Wahlman said.

He clicked off. Sat there on the bed and stared into the mirror behind the dresser. He hadn't weighed himself lately, but his face looked thinner than usual, and there were dark circles under his eyes. His hair had started graying at the temples. He was only forty years old, but some of the teenage cashiers at some of the fast food joints he went to sometimes were already starting to ask him if he qualified for the senior discount. He still felt good. Strong. But the nightmare that his life had become had taken its toll on his physical appearance.

He stripped down and took a shower, and then he pulled a clean pair of underwear out of his backpack and put them on and climbed into bed. It was early, not even nine o'clock yet, but he'd only been sleeping four or five hours a night lately, and it was starting to catch up to him.

He turned onto his side and closed his eyes. He didn't need to set the alarm clock or arrange for a courtesy call. He knew that he would wake up at the usual time, at 5:27 in the morning.

7

Kasey walked to the door and looked through the peephole. Her parents had gone into town to do some shopping—a twenty-mile trip, each way—and Natalie had gone with them, hoping to find a new bathing suit for the summer. Before leaving, Kasey's dad had called a service technician to perform some routine maintenance on the central heating and air conditioning system, and the guy had said that he was extremely busy this time of year and that it might be late into the evening hours before he could make it over.

So Kasey hadn't immediately felt uneasy about someone knocking on the door, but the guy standing on the porch didn't really look like a service technician. He was wearing a white shirt and a tan sports jacket, jeans and boots and a white cowboy hat. Dark brown hair. Mustache.

Kasey was certain that she'd never seen him before.

She was thinking about walking over to the bureau at the end of the foyer and opening the drawer and grabbing the pistol that was in there when she noticed the white van in the driveway. *JOE'S HEATING AND AIR*, the side panel said, in big brown letters. So maybe the guy on the porch was going to put some coveralls or something on before starting the work he'd come to do.

Kasey opened the door.

"Hi," she said. "My dad's not here right now, but I guess you can—"

"Are you Kasey Stielson?"

"Yes."

"I need to talk to you."

Kasey glanced over at the van. A guy wearing a gray shirt and a red ball cap climbed out and started walking toward the east side of the house, where the outside air conditioning unit was located. Then Kasey remembered what her dad had said, that the previous owners had used the same heating and air conditioning company for years and had highly recommended their services, that the guys were familiar with the setup, and that it really wasn't necessary for anyone to be home when they came and performed the annual cleaning and refrigerant check.

"What do you want?" Kasey said to the man on the porch.

"May I come in?"

"I don't think so. Are you trying to sell something, or what?"

"I'm looking for a man named Rock Wahlman."

"Never heard of him," Kasey said.

She glanced up the hill, saw a long black sedan parked along the side of the road. She took a step backward and started to close the door.

The man slid his foot between the door and the jamb.

"I'm pretty sure you have heard of him," the man said. "This is going to be a lot easier for both of us if you cooperate."

"And what if I don't cooperate?"

"I know your parents live here, and your daughter. Don't make this any more difficult than it needs to be."

"Are you threatening to do physical harm to me and my family?" Kasey said.

"Of course not," the man said. "But Rock Wahlman is wanted for murder. Anyone who helps him stay hidden from the authorities could be charged with a number of serious crimes. You, your parents, and your daughter—even though she's still a minor. Is that what you want? Do you want Natalie to spend the rest of her teenage years in a juvenile detention center?"

"Who are you?" Kasey said.

"My name's Decker. I'm a professional tracker and bounty hunter. I'm working with a private investigator from New Orleans. Guy named Feldman. He was hired by the New Orleans Police Department as a special consultant in the case against Mr. Wahlman."

"You're wasting your time," Kasey said. "I don't know where he is."

"May I come in?"

Kasey took a deep breath, and then she opened the door wide enough for Decker to cross the threshold. He took his hat off as he entered the house. He was wearing some kind of cologne or aftershave, a scent that reminded Kasey of a certain brand of floor cleaner that she'd used recently.

She led him into the living room and motioned for him to have a seat on the leather couch, and then she rolled the chair from the computer desk over to the coffee table and sat across from him. She didn't offer him a cup of coffee or even a glass of water. She wanted to get him out of there as soon as possible so she could contact Rock and warn him.

"I'm telling you, I don't know where he is," she said.

"When was the last time you talked to him?"

"He called just a little while ago. But he never tells me his exact location."

"Concerned that someone might be listening in?"

"Of course. And concerned that someone like you might show up and start asking questions."

"Does Mr. Wahlman ever tell you his approximate location?" Decker said.

"No."

"I find that hard to believe."

"I don't really give a shit what you find hard to—"

"You need to give a shit," Decker said. "If I'm not satisfied with the information gained from our little interview session here, the next person who knocks on your door will be from the state police. You and your daughter and your parents will be charged with aiding and abetting a fugitive from justice. The four of you will be taken into custody and extradited to Louisiana, where you will be given a court date. You might be released on bail, if you can afford it, but your lives will be disrupted for a long time. Months. Years maybe. Then, if you're convicted, you might be facing—"

"Natalie wasn't involved in any of this," Kasey said.

"Okay. Let's say she wasn't. She's only fourteen years old. The court's not going to let her just walk away and live independently. I understand that her father is deceased, so there's a very good chance that she would become a ward of the state. It's a heartbreaking situation. I've seen it happen more times than I care to remember. So yes, you need to give a shit about what I believe and what I don't believe. As of now, you and your family haven't been charged with anything, but that could change very quickly. All I want is Wahlman. Tell me what you know, and I'll leave you alone forever."

Tears welled in Kasey's eyes. She didn't want to see anything bad happen to Rock. She loved him. She wanted to be with him forever.

But the welfare of her daughter came first.

"He's in Missouri," she said. "He has an SUV with a fake registration. It broke down, and it's going to be a while before he can drive it again. He's staying somewhere while it's being worked on, but I don't know exactly where."

"Would you happen to know the tag number on that vehicle?" Decker said. "And the phone number he called you from a while ago?"

Kasey told him the tag number, and the phone number, and then she lost control of her emotions. She started sobbing uncontrollably, knowing in her heart that she would never see Rock Wahlman again.

8

It had been years since Wahlman's internal alarm clock had failed him, so it came as a complete shock when he opened his eyes and glanced over at the nightstand and saw that it was 8:57 in the morning.

He'd slept for about twelve hours.

He climbed out of bed and took a quick shower and headed over to the diner.

The breakfast crowd had come and gone, and he had the counter to himself again. The Waitress With No Name wasn't there. Another young lady stepped over and asked him if he would like a cup of coffee. She was petite and perky with short blonde hair and eyes the shade of robins' eggs.

The Waitress With No Name 2.

"Yes on the coffee," Wahlman said, studying the laminated menu he'd picked up on the way in. "And let me get the number four breakfast platter, with a side of hash browns."

"How do you want your eggs?"

"Fast. I'm meeting someone here in a little while, and—"

"I mean how do you want them cooked?" The Waitress

With No Name 2 said, never cracking a smile.

"Scrambled will be fine," Wahlman said. "And make the coffee a large, please."

The Waitress With No Name 2 poured some coffee into a large paper cup and set it on the counter in front of Wahlman, and then she punched his breakfast order into the computer.

"Should be out in a few minutes," she said.

"Thanks. I'm going to step outside and get a newspaper. I'll be right back."

Wahlman stepped outside and fed some coins into the machine and grabbed a paper from the top of the stack. As he was turning to head back into the diner, he saw the man he'd hired to give him a ride to Junction City.

The Boyfriend Of The Waitress with No Name stepped up onto the sidewalk. He was wearing the tan leather work boots again. They appeared to be dry now, but they were discolored up to the ankles.

Like Wahlman's.

From sloshing around in the flooded house over on Sunset.

"You ready to go?" Boyfriend said.

"You're early," Wahlman said. "I was going to eat some breakfast."

"We better get going. You wouldn't want to miss your appointment."

"Why would I miss it? Junction City's only three hours from here."

"You never know what traffic's going to be like."

Wahlman shrugged. “All right,” he said. “You mind if I eat in your truck?”

“Not at all.”

Wahlman walked inside and asked The Waitress With No Name 2 to change his order to a carryout, and a few minutes later he climbed into the truck with Boyfriend and munched on a strip of bacon as they made their way toward the interstate.

But Boyfriend didn’t take a left where he should have. He didn’t turn onto the road that led to the on-ramps. Instead, he kept going straight. Toward Fantasy.

“I think you should have turned back there,” Wahlman said.

Left-handed, and with lightning speed, like some kind of ambidextrous gunslinger from the old west, Boyfriend pulled a handgun out from the other side of the driver seat and aimed the barrel at Wahlman’s face.

“Shut up and eat your breakfast,” he said. “We’re going to take a little detour.”

9

The red and white sign mounted over the service bays said *REALITY AUTO REPAIR*. Decker steered into the parking lot, climbed out of his car, entered the building through a steel and glass swinging door that led to an enclosure with a counter and a waiting area.

A guy wearing a blue shirt with an embroidered blue and white patch that said *GERRY* over the left breast pocket was sitting behind the counter staring at a computer screen. He had oily hair that didn't appear to be quite natural in color, and a thick and gaudy pair of rhinestone-studded eyeglasses that didn't appear to be quite from this planet. Blackened fingernails, scabbed knuckles. He glanced up from his monitor and asked Decker if he could help him.

"You working on this car?" Decker said, sliding a piece of paper across the counter with the tag number Kasey Stielson had given him written on it.

Gerry picked up the piece of paper, tapped some keys on his keyboard.

"It's not ready yet," he said.

"But it's here?"

"Yeah. It's here. It's parked around back."

"I'm looking for the man who brought it in," Decker said. "Any idea where he might be staying?"

Gerry raked his greasy fingers through his greasy hair.

"Is he a friend of yours or something?" he said.

"Or something," Decker said.

"I don't know where he's staying. Not for sure. But he's probably over at The Reality Hotel."

"Where's that?"

"Right down the road. You could walk there if you wanted to."

Decker folded the piece of paper and slid it back into his pocket. He handed the mechanic a blank business card with a phone number written on it.

"Give me a call if you hear from the owner of that vehicle," he said.

"Is he in some kind of trouble or something?"

"More than you can imagine. Just give me a call if you see him or if he calls the shop."

"Okay."

Decker left the repair shop and drove to the hotel. The wormy little clerk at the check-in desk cited some sort of privacy policy, but he suddenly became much more cooperative when Decker told him that Wahlman was wanted for murder and that anyone hindering the investigation could be charged with a serious crime.

Wahlman wasn't in his room, but he hadn't checked out of the hotel, so Decker figured he would be back.

Feldman had agreed to pay Decker his normal fee for this kind of thing, but that was peanuts compared to the bounty that was out on Wahlman. Big bucks, and Decker wanted all of it. Which meant that he would have to deliver Wahlman to the NOPD himself. Which could be quite a problem with a guy that big, a guy with a history of violent confrontations, a guy determined to evade capture at all costs.

But that was okay.

Because, as of late last night, Wahlman's wanted status had been changed. He was now wanted dead or alive, and Decker had a nice big car with a nice big trunk.

He sat in the parking lot and waited.

10

The gun must have been strapped between the seat and the door. Completely out of sight from the passenger side. No way for Wahlman to have seen it when he'd climbed into the pickup. It was a .357 revolver. Wahlman had owned one similar to it when he was in the Navy. Bright stainless steel finish, rubber grips. Wahlman could see the fat tips of the magnum rounds through the holes in the cylinder.

"Where are you taking me?" Wahlman said.

"You'll see," Boyfriend said.

He took a left onto a gravel road that gradually turned to dirt after a quarter mile or so, and then he made a series of disorienting turns through the woods, finally stopping at the edge of a clearing, about fifty yards from a large wooden barn. Wahlman had been waiting for a chance to lunge over and twist the gun out of his hand, but the chance had never come. Boyfriend had kept the pistol aimed at Wahlman's core the entire time. One little hiccup, and a hole the size of a quarter would be bored through Wahlman's left bicep and into his chest. Deep into his left lung, for sure, and maybe all the way into his pericardial cavity. It was highly unlikely that he would survive such a wound, much less be able to fend off a second shot. So he hadn't made a move. Not yet. He was waiting for a mistake, or some kind of diversion. Anything that might give him an opening.

"Now what?" Wahlman said, staring straight ahead through the windshield, toward the barn.

"You'll see," Boyfriend said.

"You and your buddy tried to steal that piano, didn't you?"

"Shut up."

"Your boots gave you away. They were wet, up to the ankles, just like mine. I figured it was probably a coincidence. But I figured wrong, didn't I?"

"I guess you think you're pretty smart," Boyfriend said. "But that kind of reasoning can work both ways. My girlfriend told me that you were staring at my boots when I left the restaurant yesterday. Then she told me that your boots looked the same as mine. Wet up to the ankles. Two plus two equals four. You know? I talked to a friend later on. Brad Tingly. He's a cop. He confirmed my suspicions. You should have minded your own business. Then you wouldn't be—"

"I was a cop too," Wahlman said. "United States Navy, Master-At-Arms. It's not my nature to mind my own business, especially when I see something that's obviously wrong. Like a vacant house with the back door standing open."

"You should have kept walking."

Wahlman couldn't argue with that. He'd gotten himself into something that was going to be very difficult to get out of, all for what appeared to be some sort of theft ring.

"What's in the barn?" he said. "You and your buddy have a nice little business going here, don't you?"

"Open the door and climb out of the truck and get on the ground," Boyfriend said. "Facedown, hands behind your head. Slow and easy, if you want to keep breathing."

Wahlman didn't move.

"Why a piano?" he said. "And why right there in Reality, where you live? Seems pretty stupid to me. Almost like you were trying to get caught."

"I don't want to get blood all over my interior, but I'll shoot you where you're sitting if I have to. Out of the truck. Now."

"Was it your idea, or your buddy's idea? A Baby grand piano. I've run across some dumbass criminals in my day, but that pretty much takes the cake. I've been trying to figure out why in the world anyone would—"

"Now!" Boyfriend shouted.

He leaned over and jammed the barrel of the pistol into Wahlman's ribcage.

Which presented a potential window of opportunity.

Boyfriend was off balance now. Mentally, and physically. Which, from Wahlman's perspective, could have ended up being a very good thing, or a very bad thing. Wahlman figured he had about a fifty percent chance of successfully leaning forward and avoiding the brunt of the initial blast, perhaps only being grazed by the bullet as it whizzed by or scorched by the muzzle flash as the powder exploded out of the barrel. Then he could quickly grab the gun and break Boyfriend's arm in three or four places—and maybe crush a few facial bones while he was at it—and leave him there in the clearing writhing on the ground, hoping someone would show up to take him to the hospital.

But that wasn't what happened. Not exactly.

Just as Wahlman was about to make his move, a second pickup truck sped into the clearing, whipping around 180 degrees on the soft earth, stopping nose-to-nose with Boyfriend's truck, just a few feet away, a few feet closer to the barn.

A man climbed out of the truck. It was the guy Boyfriend had been hanging out with at the diner yesterday. Boyfriend's partner in crime, the way Wahlman had it figured. He was wearing shorts and sneakers and a muscle shirt and a ball cap backwards. He took a few steps toward Boyfriend's truck, opened the passenger side door and grabbed Wahlman by the arm.

Which was a stupid thing to do, considering that the barrel of Boyfriend's revolver was still jammed against Wahlman's ribcage.

"Get out," Partner In Crime said.

Wahlman didn't say anything.

And he didn't get out of the truck.

In a single swift and precise motion, he swung his elbow like a pendulum, knocking the barrel of the gun toward the backrest of the bucket seat, managing to lean forward, toward the dashboard, a split second before Boyfriend pulled the trigger.

There was an earsplitting blast and a simultaneous shower of blood and bone and brain tissue as the top of Partner In Crime's head exploded against the blueness of the late-spring Missouri sky.

Wahlman yanked the hot revolver from Boyfriend's hand and clouted him in the forehead with it and Boyfriend's eyes rolled back in his head and he collapsed sideways against the driver side door. His face immediately went pale, as if someone had swiped it with a brush dipped in grayish-white paint.

Wahlman leaned over and checked his pulse. It was weak and rapid and there was a rattle in his throat every time he tried to take a breath and it was doubtful that he would live much longer, with or without medical attention.

He probably wasn't going to make it, no matter what, but it wasn't in Wahlman's nature to just sit there and do nothing. He used the cell phone in Boyfriend's pocket to call 911. He made the call, but he didn't say anything. He didn't want his voice to be on the recording. He left the line open and set the phone on the center console. It would only take a couple of minutes for the operator to pinpoint the signal, and then she could send help. Under the circumstances, Wahlman felt that it was the best he could do.

Mr. Conscientious. He just hoped it wouldn't come back to bite him on the ass.

He grabbed the revolver and maneuvered his way out of the truck, careful not to step in the puddle of goo that had been a living breathing human being just a few seconds previously.

Partner In Crime's truck was still running.

And it had a full tank of gas.

Wahlman climbed in and put it in gear and headed back through the woods, toward the highway. He figured he still might be able to make his appointment in Junction City, if he hurried.

11

The hacker had wanted to meet at a certain park, at a certain time, on a certain bench. Old school. Like spies in classic movies did it sometimes. Which was fine with Wahlman. Whatever worked. Whatever would lead him to getting the information he needed.

He abandoned the pickup truck a few blocks from the park and walked the rest of the way and found the bench. It was 1:43 in the afternoon. It was a beautiful day. Warm, but not too humid. Birds were chirping and squirrels were scurrying and little kids were swinging on the swings and sliding on the slides and climbing on the jungle gyms.

Wahlman waited.

He took a deep breath. His stomach was churning, because he was getting ready to do something that could potentially get him into deeper trouble than he was already in. He was getting ready to commission an act of espionage. Which, in essence, would make him a conspirator to an act of espionage. Which would make him eligible for the death penalty, if anything went wrong.

But apparently someone in the army had already sentenced him to die anyway. Just because of who he was. Just because he was an exact genetic duplicate of a man named Jack Reacher. A military policeman whose DNA had been extracted from blood samples taken over a hundred years ago.

There had been two clones produced from those samples. Rock Wahlman, and a man named Darrell Renfro. The army had been conducting some sort of experiment, but for some reason the experiment had come to a screeching halt while Wahlman and Renfro were still toddlers. They'd been sent to different orphanages in different states. Now, almost forty years later, the army was trying to eliminate any shred of evidence that the experiment had ever taken place. Renfro had been murdered already, and Wahlman knew that he was next.

He just didn't know why.

And he needed to know why. He needed to expose the forces behind what was happening. It was the only way that he was going to be able to survive. If it meant committing what would technically amount to a capital offense, then so be it. If it meant committing a hundred such crimes, then so be it. He was all in. He was ready to go the distance. The only other real choice was to lie down and die. And that just wasn't going to happen. There was something in his DNA that would never allow that to happen. Not as long as he still had the strength to put up a fight.

At exactly two o'clock, a man carrying a brown leather briefcase walked up and sat on the wooden park bench, leaving a distance of approximately two feet between himself and Wahlman.

"Do you have a cigarette?" the man said.

The preselected code question.

Wahlman was still rattled from the ordeal with Boyfriend and Partner In Crime, and he couldn't remember if he was supposed to say yes or no. A sense of panic washed over him. He was going to blow the whole deal right off the bat. He could feel the sweat beading on his forehead. He looked at the man and shrugged.

Then it came to him.

"I don't smoke," he said. "It's bad for your health."

The man breathed a sigh of relief. "You had me worried there for a second," he said.

"Sorry," Wahlman said. "I had kind of a rough time getting here. So how is this going to work?"

"The information you asked for is in the briefcase."

"The information on Colonel Dorland? You have it already?"

"Yes. I have his real name, a copy of his service record, and an outline of his current assignment. And a map that shows the exact location of his current personal quarters and the exact location of the unit he's currently commanding."

Wahlman unzipped his jacket and pulled an envelope out of the inner pocket. The envelope contained exactly ten thousand dollars in cash, given to Wahlman by Kasey's parents. Which, in essence, made them conspirators too. Not that anyone would ever find out about their involvement. The only way anyone would ever find out was if Wahlman turned, and that wasn't going to happen.

He set the envelope on the bench, approximately halfway between where he was sitting and where the hacker was sitting.

"Take it and walk away," Wahlman said. "Leave the briefcase here."

The hacker didn't move.

"I'm going to need more than that," he said. "I'm going to need twenty."

"You said ten."

"I'm going to need twenty."

Wahlman clenched his teeth. He felt like reaching over and grabbing the hacker by the throat.

"What's stopping me from caving your skull in with my bare hands and taking the briefcase and keeping the money?" he said.

"This," the hacker said, pulling his right hand out of his pocket and revealing a stainless steel box about the size of a deck of cards. "There's a button on the box. I'm pressing it with my thumb right now. If I choose to take my thumb off the button, or if something happens that causes my thumb to be taken off the button, the briefcase will explode."

Wahlman squinted toward the little box. He figured the hacker was bluffing. Why risk your own life for a measly twenty grand? Or for any amount of money, for that matter. Wahlman figured he was bluffing, but there was no way to know for sure. Which meant that he was going to have to play ball with this guy.

"How do I know the briefcase really contains the

information you said it contains?" Wahlman said.

"Are you calling me a liar?"

"You lied about the amount of money it was going to cost me. How do I know you're not lying about everything else? You're going to have to give me something. Some kind of proof that you really—"

"Earlier this year, Dorland's unit abruptly abandoned a secret complex that had been set up in the Mojave Desert," the hacker said.

Which was true.

Wahlman knew it was true, because he'd gone into the secret complex and had looked around, after Dorland and his intelligence unit had bugged out. So maybe the hacker was legit after all. And maybe the briefcase really was rigged with explosives. It seemed odd that the hacker would be willing to blow himself up over something like this, but maybe he really needed the cash. Maybe it was for a gambling debt, or a medical procedure, or to keep his house from going into foreclosure. Wahlman supposed there were all kinds of events that might have caused the hacker to become desperate enough to risk being blown to smithereens.

"That's all the money I have," Wahlman said, gesturing toward the envelope. "I'll have to owe you the rest."

The hacker laughed. "This isn't the kind of thing you can pay for with an installment plan," he said. "Give me the money today, or the deal's off."

"How can I give you what I don't have?"

"I'm sure you'll figure it out. There's a coffee shop at the corner of First and Main. It's only a few blocks from here.

There's one of those payday loan places on the way. Maybe they can help you out. Meet me at the coffee shop in one hour. If you're not there with the money, you'll never see me again."

The hacker put his hand back in his pocket, and then he got up and walked away.

12

Wahlman put the envelope back in his pocket and zipped his jacket. He stayed there on the bench, gazing out toward the playground and wondering how he was going to come up with another ten thousand dollars in less than an hour. He thought about trying to sell the pickup truck he'd driven to Junction City. It was a nice truck. It was probably worth forty or fifty grand. Wahlman had noticed a pool hall not far from the park. He could go in there and ask around, maybe find a dirty pawnbroker who would look the other way on the paperwork.

But all that would take time, something Wahlman was extremely short of at the moment. So there was really only one way to get the money.

Wahlman got up and started walking west, toward First Street. It was uphill from the park and the day had gotten warmer and there wasn't much of a breeze and he could feel the sweat trickling down his back. He stopped in front of the payday loan place the hacker had mentioned. There was a sign taped to the window that said they had a money wiring service there as well.

Wahlman thought about it for a few more seconds, and then he pulled out his cell phone and punched in Kasey's number. She answered on the third ring.

"I need ten thousand dollars," Wahlman said.

"Unbelievable," Kasey said. "You call me on the phone, and those are the first words out of your mouth?"

"Sorry. I need it in a hurry. The man I met with a while ago has the information I need. This whole ordeal could be over in a matter of days. But I have to have the money."

"I thought Daddy already gave you what you needed for that."

"The guy I met with wants more. He wants twice the amount we originally agreed on. What can I do? I have to pay him, or he's going to disappear on me. Then I'll be back to square one."

"How do you know this guy really has the—"

"I talked to him. He knows things. I'm pretty sure he has the information I need to get to the bottom of all this. He knows about Dorland. He has a copy of his service record, and he knows where he is. And he knows his real name."

There was a long pause. Wahlman could hear whispers in the background and paper shuffling.

"Do you have a place in mind where we can wire you the money?" Kasey said.

"Yes. I'm standing outside a place right now."

"Daddy says he will do it, but that this is the last time. Okay?"

"Okay."

Another long pause.

"There are some things I need to talk to you about," Kasey said.

"What things?" Wahlman said.

"You said you're in a hurry. Go ahead and do what you need to do. We can talk later."

She hung up.

Somewhat perplexed by Kasey's attitude, but having no time to dwell on it right now, Wahlman walked into the payday loan place. A few minutes later, he added another ten thousand dollars to the envelope in his pocket, and then he headed toward the coffee shop.

13

As it turned out, Wahlman was almost twenty minutes early. The hacker wasn't there yet.

The coffee shop was not busy. Wahlman and the barista were the only people in there at the moment, and the barista behaved as though she would rather be almost anywhere else. No smile, no friendly chitchat. Just going through the motions. Maybe she wasn't always like that, Wahlman thought. Maybe she was just having a bad day. Maybe her boyfriend had broken up with her five minutes ago. No telling. Wahlman ordered a cup of coffee and sat at a table by the front window.

There was a horse-drawn carriage parked at the curb. For twenty-five bucks, the driver would take you on a fifteen-minute tour of the historic district. It was the kind of thing normal people did. People who weren't running for their lives.

Wahlman looked forward to the day when he could do things like that again. Ordinary things. Joyful things. He wanted to go to the movies. He wanted to walk into a restaurant without having to watch his back every second. He wanted to be able to use his real name again. He wanted to own things. A house. A car. He wanted to settle down with Kasey. Maybe start a family. All of that was starting to seem within reach now. He knew there was still a lot of work to do, but acquiring the information on Dorland would go a long way toward achieving his ultimate goal, toward getting his life back.

He looked at the clock on the wall over the service counter. Ten more minutes, and the briefcase would be his.

Ten more minutes.

He watched the seconds tick by, one at a time.

Nine more minutes.

Eight.

A uniformed police officer walked into the coffee shop. He sauntered up to the counter and said something to the barista. She seemed as bored and uninspired as she had when she'd waited on Wahlman. The officer seemed chipper and energetic, but he didn't appear to be in any sort of hurry. Probably working the middle shift, Wahlman thought. Probably just getting started. This was probably morning coffee for him. Maybe his first cup of the day. Maybe his only cup, depending on how many calls came in during his shift.

The barista brought the officer a paper cup with a lid on it. The officer handed her some cash, turned around and exited the shop, nodding at Wahlman on his way out. He was young. Early twenties. Two or three years on the job, at the most. Probably not a rookie, but probably not very experienced either. He waved at the driver as he walked past the carriage, and then he treaded up the hill to where his cruiser was parked.

Wahlman looked at the clock again. Three more minutes. The hacker had been punctual for the first meeting, and there was no reason to think that he wouldn't be for this one.

No reason until those three minutes ticked by and the hacker still wasn't there.

Wahlman went to the counter and bought another cup of coffee. Carried it to the table by the window and sat back down. The hacker was four minutes late now, and Wahlman was starting to get concerned. Maybe the hacker had gotten cold feet. Maybe he'd thought about it some more, and had decided against passing the information along to Wahlman after all, regardless of how much money would change hands. Maybe he'd disabled the little detonator and had thrown the briefcase off a bridge. Those were the thoughts going through Wahlman's head when the percussive wave from an enormous blast somewhere west of the coffee shop knocked him out of his chair and caused the plate glass window he had been staring out of to shatter into a million pieces.

The horse out at the curb started rearing and thrashing and the people out on the sidewalk started running and screaming.

Wahlman reached up and gripped the seat of the chair he'd been sitting on and pushed himself to a standing position. He brushed the tiny pieces of glass off his clothes and dizzily made his way to the counter to make sure the barista was okay. She was on the floor, hunkered into a corner, hugging her knees and staring blankly at a stack of paper cups that had toppled over into the sink.

"You all right?" Wahlman said.

She nodded.

Wahlman turned and staggered to the door and jerked it open and stepped out onto the sidewalk. Something was on fire, just over the hill, just beyond where the police car was parked. The cop was nowhere in sight, but the cup of coffee he'd bought was on the top of the cruiser, behind the light bar, somehow undisturbed by whatever had taken place on the other side of the hill.

There was no way for Wahlman to know exactly what had happened, but his best guess was that the hacker had done something to draw the attention of the police officer, and that the subsequent encounter had somehow led to one nervous thumb being lifted from one detonator button. Which of course had led to the explosion.

Maybe the hacker had left his car in a no parking zone or something. Maybe he'd jaywalked. Maybe the officer had recognized him from some sort of previous encounter. Wahlman had no idea, and he would never have any idea, because he didn't plan on sticking around long enough to find out.

He stared at the black plumes of a smoke rising in the air, and then he turned and started walking in the opposite direction, back down the hill, back toward the park.

14

Wahlman had been planning on taking a bus back to Reality and hiding out until the repair shop closed for the day. He'd been planning on leaving some money and finding his keys and skipping out unnoticed sometime after dark. He certainly didn't want anyone from that area to see him driving the truck he'd taken. It was possible that Boyfriend had survived the blow to the head, possible that he would wake up at some point, possible that he would eventually be coherent enough to talk to the police. Not likely, but possible. And if Boyfriend did wake up, and if he did talk to the police, there was no telling what kind of story he might tell them about his friend being shot.

So Wahlman had been planning on taking a bus, and he'd been planning on getting into and out of Reality as quickly as possible.

But things had changed.

A police officer had been killed, and Wahlman had walked away from the scene, and the melancholy barista at the coffee shop could identify Wahlman if she needed to, and that was all he needed, more trouble with the law.

So he didn't really want to hang around in Junction City long enough to take a bus, but he didn't really want to drive the pickup truck back to Reality either.

He was starting to wonder if he should just forget about the SUV. Chalk it up as a loss. Forget about it and never go anywhere near Reality, Missouri again.

He strolled into the park and sat on the same bench he'd been sitting on earlier. It had been a rough day. First the incident with Boyfriend and Partner In Crime. Then the hacker had wanted twice as much money as Wahlman had in his pocket. Then the hacker and a police officer and no telling how many innocent bystanders had been blown to bits. Not to mention the briefcase, which had supposedly contained the information Wahlman needed to start getting his life back.

At least he knew now that the information he needed was attainable. It was just a matter of time until he could find someone else to help him get it. A matter of time, and a matter of money. It had been one of the worst days of his life, but at least he knew now that the situation was not impossible.

And at least he still had Kasey.

He pulled out his cell phone and punched in her number.

"How did it go?" she said.

"It didn't," Wahlman said. "I better not elaborate over the phone, but I'm pretty much back to where I was when I started. Back when I left Tennessee."

"Do you still have the money?"

"Yes."

"Maybe you can get someone else to help you."

"That's what I was thinking," Wahlman said.

Silence for a few beats.

"I need to go," Kasey said.

"A while ago you said there was something you needed to talk to me about."

"There is, but—"

"What is it?" Wahlman said.

He could tell by Kasey's voice that she was upset about something. She sounded as though she might be on the verge of tears.

"A man was here looking for you," she said.

"What man?"

"His name is Decker. He's a professional tracker. And a bounty hunter. He's working for a private investigator. The one you got into a fight with in Bakersfield, I guess."

"Did he mention the private investigator's name?" Wahlman said.

"Feldman. I think that's what he said. Something like that."

Wahlman couldn't believe what he was hearing.

"This is all very significant," he said. "Why didn't you tell me earlier?"

"I was afraid. He started talking about aiding and abetting and the state taking Natalie away from me and—"

"You need to be afraid," Wahlman said. "Since Decker was able to find you at the lake house, it means that Dorland's people will eventually be able to find you there as well. And Dorland's people won't be interested in charging you with any sort of crime. Dorland's people will do whatever it takes to pinpoint my location. You're not safe there anymore."

"I know," Kasey said. "We packed some things and left last night."

"You left the lake house?"

"Yes. And don't ask me where we are, because I can't tell you."

"I wouldn't want you to. You know how it is with these cellular phones. You never know who might be—"

"It's not because of that," Kasey said. "This just isn't going to work out. I can't talk to you anymore. I can't see you anymore."

"What are you talking about?"

"Daddy said not to worry about the money. Keep it. Use it for whatever you need it for."

"Kasey. Listen to me. I'm getting close to resolving this thing. I can feel it. I just need a little more time. I need for you to—"

"I'm sorry. I'm really, really sorry."

"What did you say to Decker? You didn't tell him anything, did you?"

For a brief moment, Wahlman heard Kasey sobbing in the background.

Then she clicked off.

15

Wahlman sat there on the park bench for a few minutes and considered his options. He was totally alone in the world now, and—as if he didn't have enough problems to deal with already—a professional tracker named Decker was on his tail.

A tracker, and a bounty hunter.

The last time Wahlman had checked, the bounty put out on him by the New Orleans Police Department had increased to an amount that was practically unheard of. It probably wasn't quite enough for a man like Decker to retire on, but it was probably close. The online wanted posters that Wahlman had seen had specified that he was to be delivered alive and in good health, but that had been a while back. The conditions of the reward might have changed by now.

Decker was sort of a celebrity, one of those guys you see on the national news channels sometimes. *Special Investigative Consultant*, or something like that. He was known for his dogged persistence. If he was looking for you, it was only a matter of time until you were found. A fugitive had stowed away on a rocket ship to Mars one time. It didn't matter. Decker eventually caught up to him and brought him back to Earth. Decker was expensive, but he was the best. He was the guy you called when you wanted your chance of success to be one hundred percent.

Wahlman had no idea how much information Kasey had provided to Decker, but it was a pretty safe bet that Decker had squeezed her for everything he could get. Threatened her with prosecution and all that. If she'd told him everything she knew, he was probably in Reality right now. He'd probably gone to the repair shop. Maybe the hotel. Maybe the diner. Everywhere that Wahlman had been. And he was probably hanging out at one of those places and waiting for Wahlman to return.

Which ordinarily would have sent Wahlman hightailing it in the opposite direction.

But this was Decker.

He only worked for one client at a time, and he never gave up. The day he was hired, it became his sole mission in life to find Rock Wahlman and deliver him to the authorities. And that was exactly what he would do. And if the requirements for the bounty had changed, he would proceed accordingly. He wouldn't pull any punches. He would find Wahlman and ambush him and send him to Louisiana in a box.

Which meant that Wahlman needed to find him first.

Wahlman got up and slid his phone back into his pocket and started walking to where he'd parked the pickup truck. He still had the .357 revolver he'd taken from Boyfriend. It was in the glove compartment. He started the truck and eased away from the curb and made a U-turn at the first intersection he came to and headed back toward the interstate.

Back toward Reality.

16

Decker was accustomed to sitting and waiting for long periods of time. It was basically what he did for a living. Hours and hours of extreme boredom, followed by short bursts of intense excitement. The excitement part was kind of like a drug. An addiction. It was what Decker lived for.

It was almost five o'clock in the afternoon, and he hadn't eaten anything all day. And he didn't plan on eating anything until the job was done. Hunger was part of the experience. It added to the tension. The anticipation. There would be no eating—or sleeping—until Rock Wahlman was taken care of.

Decker's cell phone started vibrating. He pulled it out of his pocket and checked the caller ID. It was Feldman.

Decker didn't like to take calls while he was on a stakeout. It was a distraction. It diverted your attention from where it needed to be. It took your mind off the job at hand, and when you were the best in the world at what you did, you needed to stay focused. Every second. Because things could go very wrong in a heartbeat.

Decker usually turned the phone off, but he'd forgotten to this time.

Feldman.

Shit.

What could he possibly want?

Decker decided to go ahead and answer the call, but he was determined to keep it short.

"I'm working," he said. "What do you want?"

"Where are you?" Feldman said.

"Where I am is not important. What is important is that I'm very close to completing the job you hired me to do. Now if you'll excuse me, I would like to get back to—"

"We have a lead on a man who fits Wahlman's description."

"What kind of lead?" Decker said.

"Detective Collins called me a while ago. He and every other law enforcement officer in the country received an encrypted message from the National Terrorist Alert System. A briefcase bomb exploded in Junction City, Kansas earlier this afternoon. The paper documents that had been inside the briefcase were destroyed, but the man who had been holding the case had an interesting note tucked in his wallet."

Decker sighed. "I'm listening," he said.

"The note described a man who was very tall and very muscular, with dark brown hair and blue eyes and chiseled features. Wahlman doesn't have dark brown hair, of course, but it's very likely that he's been dying it since he's been on the run."

"What else did the note say?"

"It said that this tall and muscular man was working to obtain government secrets. He'd contacted the man with the briefcase through a mutual acquaintance, and—"

"Did the man with the briefcase have a name?" Decker said.

"His name hasn't been released yet. The note said that if anything happened to him, the tall and muscular man was to be held responsible. Then there was an apology, from whoever wrote the note—presumably the man who'd been carrying the briefcase—an apology to his family and to his colleagues and to the United States of America. It said that he was very sorry for the role he'd played in this affair, and that he hoped the people in his life could remember him for the good things he'd done."

"Sounds like the man with the briefcase was getting ready to sell some kind of classified information to the tall and muscular man," Decker said.

"Exactly," Feldman said. "But the most important part of that note, as far as we're concerned, is that it places the tall and muscular man in Junction City. That's something we can use."

"The tall and muscular man could have been anyone," Decker said.

"True. But I have a strong hunch that it was Wahlman. We're working to secure the footage from several nearby security cameras. We should know for sure by the end of the day if it was him or not."

Decker thought about that for a few seconds. It didn't really matter where Wahlman had gone that morning, or what he had done that afternoon. His primary mode of transportation was still in Reality, Missouri, and it didn't seem likely that he would just abandon it. Decker was betting that Wahlman would return to the hotel, and that it wouldn't take him much longer to get there.

"Okay," Decker said.

"That's it?" Feldman said. "Seems like you would want to—"

"Like I said, I'm working. I'll call you if I need anything, but you probably won't hear from me until the job is done."

There was a long pause.

"And when might that be?" Feldman said.

"Soon," Decker said. "Very soon."

17

Wahlman pulled over to the shoulder and switched off the ignition at approximately the same spot his SUV had stopped running yesterday. He climbed out of the pickup truck, slid the revolver into the back of his waistband. Walked to the bottom of the exit ramp again and saw the sign again and headed west toward Reality again. But he didn't walk along the side of the highway this time. He trotted across the grassy runoff that ran parallel to the road and made his way to the edge the forest.

He didn't go very deep into the woods. Just a few feet past the tree line. Just far enough from the highway to be invisible to traffic. Not that there was much, but he didn't want to take any chances. He didn't want to be seen by the police or The Waitress With No Name or the mechanic at the repair shop or the clerk at the hotel. He didn't want to be seen by the ordinary folks traveling from Reality to Fantasy, or from Fantasy to Reality, and he didn't want to be seen by anyone who had taken the wrong exit and was now lost somewhere between the two. He didn't want to be seen by anyone. He wanted to sneak into town and take Decker by surprise.

If Decker was indeed there waiting for him.

Which was a good possibility, but not a certainty.

If Decker wasn't there, Wahlman would go back to his original plan. He would wait until it was dark outside and break into the repair shop and get his keys and haul ass. But if Decker was there, he needed to take care of that situation first.

Walking as quickly as he could through the tangles of wild vegetation, it took him about thirty minutes to make it to the town limit sign. He kicked away some of the underbrush and sat down and leaned against the trunk of a pine tree and waited for the sun to go down. It took a while. Over an hour. When the first stars started showing over the horizon, he got up and put his Navy watch cap on and followed the highway into town. It wasn't nearly cold enough to be wearing the wool toboggan, but Wahlman figured it would keep the streetlights from reflecting off his forehead. He needed to keep a low profile, and he figured every little bit would help.

He crept around in the shadows and made his way to the auto repair shop. There was a light on in the office. A guy was sitting there at the counter with a stack of receipts. Finishing his paperwork for the day. Wahlman could see him through the big plate glass window in front. It was the guy with the weird glasses, the same guy Wahlman had handed a hundred dollars in cash to yesterday, to expedite the repair on his SUV. With everything that had happened since then, Wahlman had forgotten about that little detail. But now he remembered. Maybe Mr. Conscientious wouldn't leave any money on the counter after all.

The doors to the service bays had been secured for the night, and Wahlman's SUV was parked in a fenced-off area adjacent to the office. Which probably meant that the work on it had been completed.

Probably, but Wahlman needed to know for sure. He ducked behind a bush at the far end of the parking lot, pulled out his cell phone and punched in the number on the business card he'd been given yesterday. The man sitting at the counter answered the call.

"Reality Auto Repair," the man said.

"Just checking to see if my car is ready yet," Wahlman said.

"Which one is yours?"

"The white SUV."

"Yeah, it's ready. You're going to need a new battery soon. We can go ahead and take care of that for you first thing in the morning if you want us to."

"Okay," Wahlman said.

"I'll add it to the work order. You should be good to go by nine, if not sooner."

"I'll give you a call in the morning before I come, just to make sure," Wahlman said, knowing that he wouldn't really give the man a call in the morning, or ever again, knowing that he and his vehicle would be hundreds of miles away by the time the shop opened for another day of business, whether Decker was in town or not.

"You're staying at The Reality Hotel, right?" the man sitting at the counter said, his voice taking on a tone of congeniality Wahlman hadn't noticed before. Like an old friend who wanted to meet for a cocktail or something.

Wahlman didn't answer the question. He wondered why the man was suddenly interested in where he was going to sleep tonight. It was an odd thing for a mechanic to ask a customer.

Extremely odd.

Wahlman clicked off and slid the phone into his pocket and walked across the parking lot and entered the office. The man sitting at the counter still had the landline receiver he'd been talking into in one hand and he was punching a number into the keypad on the base of the phone with the other. Wahlman grabbed him by his greasy shirt and pulled him across the countertop and slammed him on the floor and pressed the barrel of Boyfriend's revolver against his forehead.

"Did someone come here looking for me?" Wahlman said.

The man's eyes got big and his lips curled into an extreme frown.

"Please don't kill me," he said. "I don't know anything about anything."

"Did someone come here looking for me?" Wahlman repeated.

"He gave me a number to call. It's on the counter. I don't know anything about anything. I was just trying to—"

"What did he want?"

"He asked me where you were staying. I told him I didn't know for sure, but that most likely you would be at the—"

"What kind of car was he driving?"

"It was a sedan. Black, with tinted windows. I'm not sure of the make and model. Seems like I would know, being a mechanic and all, but cars look so much alike these days it's hard to—"

"Shut up."

Wahlman grabbed the telephone the man had been using and ripped the cord out of the wall and used it to tie the man's wrists and ankles.

There was a patch sewn to the man's shirt, just above the breast pocket. It said *GERRY*. Wahlman hadn't noticed it before. If he remembered correctly, Gerry had been wearing a plain white t-shirt yesterday. Maybe all of his shirts with nametags had been at the cleaners or something.

"You can't just leave me here like this," Gerry said. "There won't be anyone here until seven o'clock in the morning."

"Would you prefer I leave you here unconscious?" Wahlman said. "Because that can definitely be arranged."

Silence.

Wahlman ferreted through the papers on the counter until he found a blank business card with a phone number written on it.

Then he exited the office and walked back out into the night.

18

It only took Wahlman a few minutes to walk to the hotel. He saw the black sedan in the parking lot right away, but he didn't know if Decker was inside the car or not. The car was too far away, and the windows were too heavily tinted.

Wahlman crouched behind the sculpted row of hedges growing along the edge of the sidewalk and considered his options. He had a hunch that his status had changed from *Wanted: Alive and Healthy* to *Wanted: Dead or Alive.* As a general rule, Decker didn't take cases that required suspects to be breathing when they were brought into custody. As a general rule, he would petition for your status to be downgraded if need be, and then he would stalk you until he found you.

And then he would gun you down with no warning.

That kind of aggressive—and in Wahlman's opinion, barbaric—method of law enforcement had been made possible by the Capital Crime Control Act of 2087. Wahlman had been a Master-At-Arms in the United States Navy at the time, and had been bound by the Uniform Code of Military Justice, so he'd never been in a position to deal with the controversial legislation firsthand, but he'd voiced his opposition to it in letters to elected officials, and it was one of the reasons he'd never signed on to work for a state or city law enforcement agency after leaving the Navy.

It was a bad law. It allowed people like Decker to cash in on people like Wahlman for the price of a bullet. All it took was a judge's signature on the bounty decree. Then it was open season on your ass. It was a terrifying direction the country had gone in, and Wahlman hoped someone would put a stop to it soon.

But nobody was going to put a stop to it tonight.

Which didn't give Wahlman much of a choice about what he needed to do next.

He pulled Boyfriend's .357 from the back of his waistband, stood and stepped over the hedge and started walking across the parking lot, toward the black sedan. He stopped when he was about thirty feet away from it.

The driver side door opened and Decker climbed out.

He had a pistol in his hand.

He pointed it in Wahlman's direction.

"On the ground," he shouted. "I'm not going to tell you twice."

Wahlman pointed the revolver in Decker's direction.

"You get on the ground," Wahlman said. "I'm not going to tell you twice either."

"You're coming with me," Decker said. "I can cuff you and put you in the back seat, or I can kill you and put you in the trunk. Either way is fine with me."

Before Wahlman could respond, a pair of RPD cruisers squealed around the corner, screeching to a stop in the area between where Wahlman was standing and where Decker was standing.

Two uniformed officers climbed out of the car closest to Wahlman, and two more climbed out of the car closest to Decker.

The two officers closest to Wahlman aimed shotguns at him and told him to drop his weapon and get on the ground.

He dropped his weapon and got on the ground.

He didn't have a choice.

The two officers closest to Decker did likewise on that side. They told Decker to drop his weapon and get on the ground.

"I'm a professional tracker," Decker said. "My credentials are in the—"

"Drop it," one of the officers shouted. "Now!"

Wahlman heard Decker's pistol hit the pavement. Two minutes later, Wahlman and Decker had been cuffed and shackled and were now standing next to each other against one of the police cars.

The other cruiser was parked directly in front of them. Someone was sitting in the back, on the passenger side. One of the officers opened the door, and a man climbed out.

A man with tan leather work boots and a bloodstained shirt and a big bruise on his forehead.

19

A third cruiser steered into the parking lot, and then a fourth. Now there were eight cops on the scene.

Boyfriend's hands were cuffed behind his back. Wahlman guessed that he'd been taken to the hospital, and that the police had found the barn full of stolen property while investigating the shooting death of Partner In Crime.

A shooting death that would now be blamed on Wahlman.

He would be taken into custody, and it would only be a matter of time until the Reality Police Department found out that his driver's license and vehicle registration were fake, and it would only be a matter of time until they learned his true identity and the troublesome baggage that went along with it.

If the RPD did a good job with their investigation—with interrogation and forensics and ballistics and so forth—it might eventually be proven that Boyfriend actually fired the shot that killed his friend. It was possible that Wahlman would be exonerated for that particular crime, but whether he was or wasn't, he would eventually be extradited to

Louisiana, where he would be forced to face the charges that had been brought against him there.

Big case, lots of publicity.

Wahlman was an obvious flight risk, so there would be no chance for him to get out on bail. His general location would be known to the public, and Colonel Dorland would find a way to get to him. Make it look like an accident, or maybe a gang-related hit. A shank to the gut while he was sleeping or standing in the chow line. Dorland had the resources to make something like that happen.

Which basically meant that Wahlman's life was over.

One of the officers took a couple of steps closer to where Boyfriend was standing.

"Well?" the officer said.

"That's him," Boyfriend said. "That's the man who shot Vernon."

"Which one?"

The officer was now standing about an arm's length from where Boyfriend was standing. The officer looked familiar. Short and round and balding. Wahlman squinted, focused in on his nametag. It was Sergeant Tingly, from yesterday. He'd shaved his mustache. Maybe he'd gotten tired of combing the doughnut crumbs out of it.

Wahlman stared down at the pavement for a few seconds, trying to think of a way to get out of this. But there was no way. This was it. The end of the line.

"I don't have time for this shit," Decker said. "Take these chains off of me right now, or I'm going to—"

"Shut up," Tingly said.

"Do you even know who I am? You're going to be in deep shit when I get through with you. Heads are going to roll. I can tell you that right now."

Tingly shrugged. He sidestepped a little closer to Boyfriend. Now they were almost shoulder to shoulder.

"Which one?" Tingly repeated.

Wahlman looked up and gazed directly into Boyfriend's eyes. He saw anger. Fear. A need for revenge.

And maybe just a little bit of gratitude.

If Wahlman hadn't called 911, it was very likely that Boyfriend would have died. A lot of things had gone wrong for Boyfriend over the past ten hours or so. His career as a thief was over now, and his life was in shambles, and he would be dealing with some very serious problems for a long time to come.

But at least he was alive.

And the fact that Wahlman had played a part in that was the only possible explanation for what happened next.

"That one," Boyfriend said, gesturing toward Decker. "He was the one who killed my friend. Shot him right in the head. I saw it with my own two eyes."

An expression of astonishment washed over Decker's face.

"Bullshit," he shouted. "I don't even know what he's talking about."

Two of the officers grabbed Decker and forced him into the back of the fourth cruiser that had shown up.

Tingly pulled a set of keys out of his utility belt and walked over to where Wahlman was standing.

"I could still take you in if I wanted to," Tingly said, unlocking the handcuffs and the ankle cuffs and the chain connecting the two. "You realize that, right?"

Wahlman nodded. He'd been holding the .357 revolver when the police showed up. That was a crime in itself. And he'd been pointing it at Decker's chest. Which was an even bigger crime.

But Sergeant Tingly and his crew had apprehended a suspect in a murder case. A suspect that had been unequivocally identified by an eyewitness. Decker would get off. There was no doubt about that. But right now Tingly was probably thinking that he and his guys had solved the case, and that they'd done it in a matter of hours. It was the kind of thing that led to big pats on the back from the chief. It was the kind of thing that led to promotions.

So right now, in Tingly's mind, Wahlman had helped the Reality Police Department capture a killer. Tingly wasn't going to arrest Wahlman. He was more likely to recommend him for a medal or something. Those notions would undoubtedly change by morning, but Wahlman would be long gone by then.

"So I'm free to go now?" Wahlman said.

"We're going to need a written statement. Are you still staying here at the hotel?"

"Yes."

"We can do it here, or we can do it at the station."

"Here would be good," Wahlman said.

"All right. A couple of our guys will come by your room in an hour or so. We have your driver's license on file now, so—"

"Don't worry," Wahlman said. "I'm not going anywhere."

But of course that was a lie.

Wahlman didn't know exactly where he was going, or what he was going to do when he got there, but he planned on being as far away from Reality as possible by the time the officers knocked on his door.

20

Wahlman got his things out of his room and left the hotel without checking out. He walked over to the repair shop and entered the office. Gerry was still on the floor where Wahlman had left him.

"I want to pay you for the work you did on my car," Wahlman said.

"Untie me and we'll call it even," Gerry said.

"Not going to happen. What was the total on the fuel pump replacement?"

"A million dollars."

Wahlman walked over and rested his right foot on Gerry's right kneecap. Lightly. Just to send a message. Gerry told him the real total. Parts and labor and sales tax. Wahlman counted out some cash and slapped it on the counter.

"I subtracted the hundred dollars you tried to scam me out of," Wahlman said. "Where are my keys?"

"Behind the counter. Top drawer."

Wahlman walked behind the counter and found his keys.

He went outside and climbed into the SUV and started it and took a right out of the parking lot, toward the interstate. When he got to the turnoffs for the on-ramps, he decided to go east, for no particular reason. It was a random choice. He had nowhere to go. Nobody to see. He'd been through the wringer on multiple occasions, and he was no closer to achieving his goal that when this whole thing had started.

And apparently the woman he loved was out of the picture now. He wanted to hear the sound of her voice. Touch her. Kiss her. Hold her in his arms. He longed for her, and it broke his heart to know that he might never see her again.

He realized—from a logical standpoint—that it was probably for the best. It was totally understandable that Kasey had chosen the safety of her family and herself over trying to maintain a romantic relationship with a man in Wahlman's situation.

But it still hurt.

It was almost more than he could bear.

He traveled fifty miles or so, and then he exited the interstate and took some side roads and some two-lane highways, continuing east for the most part, ending up at a truck stop somewhere between Bowling Green, Kentucky, and Nashville, Tennessee. He bought some gas, and then he walked inside, past the souvenir stand and into the restaurant area, which smelled like greasy meat and mop water.

He sat at the counter. A waitress came and asked him if he wanted coffee and he said yes. The waitress had a nametag. Her name was Sally. She brought the coffee in a ceramic mug.

"You want something to eat?" she said.

"No thanks," Wahlman said.

"You're going to need something. You can't drive all night on an empty stomach."

"How did you know I'm going to be driving all night?"

"Almost everyone who comes in here is going to be driving all night."

Wahlman shrugged.

"I guess I'll take a cheeseburger," he said.

"Fries?"

"Okay."

Sally walked to the other side of the counter and punched the order into a computerized cash register.

Wahlman sat there and stared into the oily blackness of the coffee in front of him. He was tired. Beat. He didn't know what he was going to do next. He thought about how close he was to the lake house, where Kasey and her parents and her daughter had been staying. Less than a hundred miles, probably. He thought about driving down there. Maybe Kasey and Natalie and Dean and Betsy hadn't really left yet. Maybe he and Kasey could work things out, somehow.

No.

He needed to leave her alone. He needed to honor her wishes. Trying to force the issue would only make matters worse. He needed to accept the fact that he would never see or talk to Kasey Stielson again for the rest of his life. He needed to move on.

Sally brought the food.

"There you go," she said. "Let me know if you need anything else."

"Thanks," Wahlman said.

He took a bite of the burger. It was good. Everything tasted fresh. The meat, the bun, the lettuce leaves, the tomato slices. Even the pickle wedge on the side of the plate was top-notch. The fries were crispy and seasoned just right, and Sally was there with a steaming decanter every time the coffee in his cup started getting low. Rock Wahlman had traveled all over the world during his career in the Navy, and he could honestly say that the food on the plate in front of him was some of the best he'd ever eaten—anywhere.

He finished his meal and paid Sally and left her a nice tip and got a cup of coffee to go. Walked out to the SUV and climbed inside and started the engine. He needed a new driver's license and a different automobile. He couldn't continue being the same man he'd been in Reality, Missouri, and he couldn't continue driving the same vehicle. Within forty-eight hours, every law enforcement agency in the country would have a copy of his current license and all the details on the SUV. It was only a matter of time until a cop spotted him and pulled him over.

New credentials would cost some money.

But he had some money.

He had twenty thousand dollars in his pocket.

He would eventually find a way to pay Kasey's parents back, even though they had said not to worry about it. He would pay them back, but right now he needed the cash to continue doing what he was doing. He would basically be starting from scratch, and he would be totally on his own now. But that was okay. He would dig deep and find a way to carry on.

It was what he did.

It was who he was.

It was in his blood.

Thanks so much for reading .357 SUNSET!

For occasional updates and special offers, please visit my website and sign up for my newsletter.

My Nicholas Colt thriller series includes nine full-length novels: COLT, LADY 52, POCKET-47, CROSSCUT, SNUFF TAG 9, KEY DEATH, BLOOD TATTOO, SYCAMORE BLUFF, and THE REACHER FILES: FUGITIVE (Previously Published as ANNEX 1).

THE REACHER FILES: VELOCITY takes the series in a new direction, and sets the stage for THE BLOOD NOTEBOOKS.

And now, for the first time, 4 NICHOLAS COLT NOVELS have been published together in a box set at a special low price.

All of my books are lendable, so feel free to share them with a friend at no additional cost.

All reviews are much appreciated!

Thanks again, and happy reading!

Jude

Made in the USA
Lexington, KY
13 May 2019